P9-DGG-078

DISCARD

Otis

AND THE

Puppy

Otis

LOREN LONG

PHILOMEL BOOKS · AN IMPRINT OF PENGUIN GROUP (USA) INC.

AND THE

Puppy

It was springtime on the farm where the friendly little tractor named Otis lived. The flowers bloomed, the trees were filled with leaves, and the farm buzzed with the joy of a new season. There were fields to plow and crops to plant, and Otis was right in the middle of it all, working hard, *putt puff puttedy chuff.*

When the workday was over, Otis, the little calf, and all their farm friends loved to play hide-and-seek. Otis loved to be "it," counting one-*putt*, two-*puff*, three-*puttedy* four-*chuff* as his friends ran to hide. When he reached ten, it was game on and Otis motored here and there looking for his friends.

He found the little calf hiding in a deep thicket of wildflowers.
He found the ducks hiding in Mud Pond.

And he found the bull hiding in the haystack.

Otis and the animals would play until the sun disappeared behind
the trees, making sure to be home before darkness fell.

One evening, the farmer gathered everyone up in front of the barn and gently placed a burlap sack on the ground. The sack began to wobble, tumble, and roll. It sat up, stretched to the sky, and went *Arrhhr . . . arrhhr . . . arrhf!* What could be in there?

Then out popped a little head . . .

. . . a puppy!

The puppy shook his ears, raised his head to the sky, and yelped out another *Arrhhr . . . arrhhr . . . arrhf!* Then he burst out of the sack and romped around, greeting everyone with wet kisses.

He wriggled from head to toe and his spotted tail
wiggled and wagged, wagged and wiggled.

The farm animals smiled as they watched their
happy new friend.

And then, as quickly as he had jumped out of the
sack, he wobbled over to Otis, leaned on his tire,
yawned, slouched, and plopped off to sleep.

The farmer put an old doghouse in front of the barn, scooped up the sleepy puppy, placed him in his new home, and said, "Good night, little pup."

Otis, the little calf, and all the animals filed into the barn for a good night's sleep. Otis yawned and nestled into his stall. He was thrilled to have the little puppy on the farm and he smiled as he drifted off to sleep . . . *putt puff puttedy-zzzZZZZ.*

All of a sudden he awoke to a pitiful whimper. The whimper turned into a whine and the whine into a yelp. It was the puppy!

It was dark as midnight. Otis took a deep breath, clicked on his headlights, and *putted* out to the doghouse, where he found the puppy trembling with fear. He was afraid of the dark! With a *chuff*, Otis invited him into the barn, where the puppy curled up and fell fast asleep.

From that night on, the puppy would slink from his doghouse into the barn with Otis, where he felt safe.

And after a day of working on the farm, the two friends would play hide-and-seek with the others.

One day while it was Otis's turn to be "it," he sat counting
to ten while the others hid. One-*putt*, two-*puff*, three-*puttedy*
four-*chuff* . . .

But the puppy had something else on his mind. . . .

Otis finished counting, peeled out, and
motored here and there, *putt puff puttedy chuff*,
swerving and darting and skidding as fast as he
could to find his friends.

He found the little calf hiding
behind the old apple tree.

And the ducks hiding in a scraggly growth of honeysuckle.

And he found the massive bull trying his best to hide behind a lone dandelion.

But where was the puppy?

Otis and the animals searched high and low. Even the farmer came to help.

But they couldn't find the puppy anywhere.

Finally the farmer stopped the search. "It's gettin' dark," he
said. "Let's continue the search in the morning light."
By the time they reached the barn, it was already quite late
and all the animals went right to bed.

Yet Otis couldn't sleep.

His heart ached deep inside his engine. He knew how scared of the dark his new friend was and he was worried that the puppy had wandered into the forest.

He putted over to the barn door, looked out into the night, and sighed.

Like the little puppy, Otis, too, was afraid of the dark.

But he knew what he had to do.

He clicked on his headlights and *puffed*
out into the night.

Just inside the forest, Otis stopped dead in his tracks. The sounds of the night crackled, thumped, and croaked all around him.

His heart pounded and he shook like a leaf. Every part of him wanted to turn and run back to the farm. Yet he knew his friend needed him. So he closed his eyes and began to count . . . one-*putt*, two-*puff*, three-*puttedy* four-*chuff* . . .

By the time he got to five, Otis felt a lot calmer.

When he hit ten, it was game on!

He peeled out and motored here and there. He swerved and darted and skidded and flashed his headlights everywhere in the dark night. He circled and crisscrossed the forest, making sure to see every possible place a puppy could hide.

Finally, his light shined across an old hollow log with a little
spotted tail poking out of one end.

The puppy was whimpering softly, too scared to come out, but
when he heard Otis, he squealed with joy . . . *Arrhhr, arrhhr, arrhf!*
He wriggled and wagged and wiggled right out of that log.

He squealed and cried and covered Otis's face with kisses.

Then the two friends began to make their way home. They stood tall together as they passed through the dark forest. And somehow the night sounds no longer felt so frightening to them.

On the farm, a warm safe bed awaited them.

Before long a new day would arrive, full of bright sunshine, work, and play.

THE END

To Elle and Moon, the puppies in my studio,
and to the humans that love them.

Other books in the Otis series:
Otis
Otis and the Tornado
and
Otis Loves to Play

PHILOMEL BOOKS
A division of Penguin Young Readers Group. Published by The Penguin Group.
Penguin Group (USA) Inc., 375 Hudson Street, New York, NY 10014, U.S.A.
Penguin Group (Canada), 90 Eglinton Avenue East, Suite 700, Toronto, Ontario M4P 2Y3, Canada (a division of Pearson Penguin Canada Inc.).
Penguin Books Ltd, 80 Strand, London WC2R 0RL, England.
Penguin Ireland, 25 St. Stephen's Green, Dublin 2, Ireland (a division of Penguin Books Ltd).
Penguin Group (Australia), 250 Camberwell Road, Camberwell, Victoria 3124, Australia (a division of Pearson Australia Group Pty Ltd).
Penguin Books India Pvt Ltd, 11 Community Centre, Panchsheel Park, New Delhi - 110 017, India.
Penguin Group (NZ), 67 Apollo Drive, Rosedale, Auckland 0632, New Zealand (a division of Pearson New Zealand Ltd).
Penguin Books (South Africa) (Pty) Ltd, 24 Sturdee Avenue, Rosebank, Johannesburg 2196, South Africa.
Penguin Books Ltd, Registered Offices: 80 Strand, London WC2R 0RL, England.

Edited by Michael Green.   Design by Semadar Megged. Text set in 15.5-point Engine.   The art was created in gouache and pencil.

Library of Congress Cataloging-in-Publication Data
Long, Loren.   Otis and the puppy / Loren Long.   p. cm.   Summary: When a puppy gets lost while playing hide-and-seek on the farm, Otis the friendly little tractor must face his fear of the darkness in order to help his new friend.   [1. Fear of the dark—Fiction. 2. Tractors—Fiction. 3. Dogs—Fiction. 4. Animals—Infancy—Fiction. 5. Farm life—Fiction.] I. Title.   PZ7.L8555Otp 2013   [E]—dc23   2012013312

ISBN 978-0-399-25469-7   10 9 8 7 6 5 4 3 2 1